The
Little Red Hen

Illustrated by Lilian Obligado

A GOLDEN BOOK • NEW YORK

Western Publishing Company, Inc., Racine, Wisconsin 53404

Once there was a Little Red Hen who lived
in a barnyard with her three chicks and a Duck,
a Pig, and a Cat.

One day the Little Red Hen found some grains of wheat.

"Look, look!" she clucked. "Who will help me plant this wheat?"

"Not I," quacked the Duck, and he waddled away.
"Not I," oinked the Pig, and he trotted away.
"Not I," mewed the Cat, and he padded away.

"Then I will plant it myself,"
said the Little Red Hen.

And she did.

When the wheat was tall and golden, the Little Red Hen knew it was ready to be cut.

"Who will help me cut the wheat?" she asked.

"Not I," said the Duck.
"Not I," said the Pig.
"Not I," said the Cat.

"Then I will cut the wheat myself,"
said the Little Red Hen.

And she did.

"Now," said the Little Red Hen, "it is time to take the wheat to the miller so he can grind it into flour. Who will help me?"

"Not I," said the Duck.
"Not I," said the Pig.
"Not I," said the Cat.

"Then I will have to take the wheat to
the miller myself," said the Little Red Hen.
And she did.

The miller ground the wheat into fine white
flour and put it into a sack for the Little Red Hen.

When she returned to the barnyard, the Little Red Hen asked, "Who will help me make this flour into dough?"

"Not I," said the Duck, the Pig, and the Cat all at once.

"Then I will make the dough myself,"
said the Little Red Hen.
  And she did.

When the dough was ready to go into the oven, the Little Red Hen asked, "Who will help me bake the bread?"

"Not I," said the Duck.
"Not I," said the Pig.
"Not I," said the Cat.

"Then I will bake it myself,"
said the Little Red Hen.
  And she did.

Soon the bread was ready. As she took it from the oven, the Little Red Hen asked, "Well, who will help me eat this warm, fresh bread?"

"I will!" said the Duck.
"I will!" said the Pig.
"I will!" said the Cat.

"No, you won't," said the Little Red Hen. "You wouldn't help me plant the seeds, cut the wheat, go to the miller, make the dough, or bake the bread. Now my three chicks and I will eat this bread ourselves!"

And that's just what they did.